Ponies to the Rescue

www.**kids**at**randomhouse**.co.uk

For fun, games and lots, lots more visit
www.**katiesperfectponies**.co.uk

For Katie Price's adult website visit
www.**katieprice**.co.uk

PONIES TO THE RESCUE
A BANTAM BOOK 978 0 553 82073 7

First published in Great Britain by Bantam,
an imprint of Random House Children's Books
A Random House Group Company

This edition published 2007

1 3 5 7 9 10 8 6 4 2

Set in 14/21pt Bembo MT Schoolbook

Bantam Books are published by Random House Children's Books,
61–63 Uxbridge Road, London W5 5SA

www.**kids**at**randomhouse**.co.uk
www.rbooks.co.uk

Addresses for companies within The Random House Group Limited
can be found at: www.randomhouse.co.uk/offices.htm

THE RANDOM HOUSE GROUP Limited Reg. No. 954009
A CIP catalogue record for this book is available from the British Library.

Printed in the UK by CPI Bookmarque, Croydon, CR0 4TD

Ponies to the Rescue

Illustrated by Dynamo Design

Bantam Books

Vicki's Riding School

Vicki

Jess and Rose

Cara and Taffy

Amber and Stella

Sam and Beanz

Mel and Candy

Henrietta and President

Darcy and Duke

Chapter 1

Darcy smiled as she fixed the glittering golden star to the top of the Christmas tree. It nearly touched their sitting-room ceiling!

"OK, Dad, you can put the lights on now," she called.

Her dad grinned as he flicked the switch. "One, two, three . . . blast off!" he said with a laugh.

Darcy and her mum gasped happily as the lights twinkled all over the huge tree.

Darcy's little sister, Annabelle, ran into the room carrying a present wrapped in pink and silver wrapping paper. "For me?" she shouted excitedly.

"No! Give it here, Belle," Darcy laughed, quickly running over to snatch the present from her sister's dirty hands.

"What's the panic, sweetheart?" asked her dad. "Don't worry – it's still wrapped perfectly so the surprise isn't spoiled!"

Darcy put the shiny present carefully under the Christmas tree. "No, no. It's not for any of you anyway," she told him. "It's Duke's Christmas present. I've got him a new saddle rug."

Her dad shook his head. "You think about that pony more than anybody else in the world," he teased.

Darcy ran over and gave him a hug, then put her arm round Annabelle and sat on the sofa, pulling her sister onto her knee. "I love you, Mum and Belle *nearly* as much as I love Duke," she giggled, and gave Annabelle a kiss.

It was true. She totally adored Duke, her gorgeous dark bay pony. She'd got him for her birthday just over a year ago, and not only was he gentle, he was also brave. When it came to jumping, nothing seemed to bother him, and he loved it even more than Darcy did. They made a great team. Getting Duke had been a dream come true

and Darcy now spent
every single spare
moment with
him.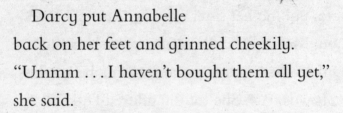

"So where
are *our*
Christmas
presents,
darling?" her
mum asked.

Darcy put Annabelle
back on her feet and grinned cheekily.
"Ummm . . . I haven't bought them all yet,"
she said.

"You'd better be quick about it –
Christmas is only five days away," her dad
told her with a laugh.

Darcy clapped her hands together
excitedly and spun round in a circle, making
her long brown plait fly out behind her.

"I know. I can't wait!" she said happily.

As Darcy's mum drove her to the stables the next morning, Darcy thought how lucky she was. She had her own gorgeous pony and a brilliant bunch of friends at Vicki's Riding School, where she kept Duke at livery. Darcy would've really liked to look after him herself all the time but there was no way her parents would let her do that. She had a long journey to school every day, and she and her parents didn't have time to feed, groom and turn Duke out in the mornings, so they paid Vicki to do it for them instead.

Darcy sometimes felt a bit guilty that she was lucky enough to have her own pony. Her friends Jess, Amber, Sam, Mel and Cara didn't have their own, even though they loved ponies just as much as she did. They'd all worked hard round the stables to prove to Vicki how dedicated they were and so she had given them each one of her ponies to look after as if it was their own.

Jess, who was the leader of the group, now looked after Rose, a stunning grey Connemara with a long silver mane and tail. Jess's best friend, Amber, the cleverest of the girls, rode gentle Stella, a black Highland pony with a striking white blaze. Mel, who was small and tough, rode the liveliest pony in the yard, a fabulous little chestnut Arab mare called Candice – Candy for short. Ginger-haired, freckly Sam, who was the joker of the gang, perfectly matched crazy Beanz, a skittish skewbald New Forest cross, and blonde-haired Cara, the shyest of all the girls, looked after Taffy, a steady palomino Welsh with a creamy-coloured mane and tail.

All the girls helped out at the yard, and they had lots of fun doing it! Darcy had never heard any of her friends complain. Whether they had to tidy the muck heap, sweep the yard, wash out feed bins, clean tack or stack hay bales, they did it with a smile – they just couldn't get enough of it!

They were totally different from the two snotty livery girls that Darcy shared a stable block with. Henrietta Reece-Thomas and Camilla Worthington didn't do anything to help. Darcy couldn't stand either of them; she definitely preferred to hang out with Jess, Amber, Sam, Mel and Cara.

As Darcy got out of the car at Vicki's stables, she was  surprised to see Mel cycling out of the yard. "Hey! Where you going?" she called.

7

Mel sneezed loudly before she could answer. "I'm going home. I feel terrible," she said in a croaky voice. Her face was hot and flushed and her eyes were streaming.

"You *look* terrible," Darcy said, feeling really sorry for her friend.

Mel sneezed again and pulled a tissue out so she could blow her nose. "Thanks, mate!" she said, trying to laugh. "I feel *well* bad letting Vicki down on a Saturday morning though."

Darcy nodded. She knew exactly what Mel meant. Saturday mornings were always mad at Vicki's Riding School: children from four to twelve years old arrived every hour all through the morning for their weekly riding lessons.

Darcy gave Mel a hug. "Don't worry – I can help out instead of you this morning," she offered.

Mel smiled weakly. "Thanks, Darcy,

you're wicked," she said gratefully.

Darcy ran towards the stables, where Jess, Amber, Sam and Cara were grooming their ponies in the winter sunshine. When they heard that Darcy was going to help out, they all looked relieved.

"Phew! Thanks a lot, Darcy," said Jess. "We were getting a bit stressed out here!"

"No problem." Darcy smiled at them. "But first I've got to feed Duke! I'll be as quick as I can," and she ran across the yard to Duke's stable.

Duke was already on the lookout for Darcy! His handsome dark head was stuck over his half-open stable door and he was snorting impatiently. When he saw her, he neighed loudly.

"Hello, babe," Darcy called as she opened his door.

Duke pushed his soft warm muzzle into Darcy's tummy and nudged her affectionately. "Who's the most beautiful pony in the world?" she whispered in his ear.

Duke looked up and blew in her face, then he neighed loudly as if to say, *Well . . . me of course!*

While Duke stuffed his face with a bucket of pony nuts, Darcy quickly brushed him down and picked out his feet. When he'd finished his breakfast, she untied his lead rope, which she'd bought with the pocket money she'd saved up last year, then led him across the yard to the field. Darcy knew Duke would be happy to spend the morning there while she helped out with the riding lessons.

Back at the yard, the young riders were already arriving for their lessons. Some were so little they had to be lifted onto their ponies; some were shy or nervous and some were really noisy and over-enthusiastic. But they all had one thing in common – they wanted to learn to ride, and this hour was the highlight of their week.

Vicki watched them all carefully. She was firm and sometimes strict but she was kind too, and she always tried to make lessons fun. Everybody loved Vicki. She was slim, with lovely dark hair and tanned skin, *and* she was an amazing rider. The girls often wondered if there was anything she couldn't do! Vicki adored all her horses and ponies, but she had a special soft spot for her two oldest ponies. She'd had them since she was a little girl.

Dumpling, a dark bay Shetland pony – who, at twenty-four, was nearly as old as Vicki – and fifteen-year-old Flora, a light bay Dartmoor, were Vicki's babies! Nothing would ever persuade her to get rid of either of them, and the young riders loved them almost as much as she did. Though Dumpling was old and a bit chubby now, she was still a good jumper when she could be bothered. But these days she preferred

 grazing in the pony meadow and rolling on her back in the muddy patch by the stream. Every Saturday morning the youngest riders argued about who was going to ride which pony, and Dumpling was always one of the favourites.

It was Ben's turn on Dumpling this week and Darcy helped him into the saddle. Bill and Ben were a pair of naughty little twins who loved nothing better than showing off all through their riding lessons. Even Dumpling looked cross with Ben today and she started to stamp her feet.

"Pack it in, Ben. Dumpling's an old lady and you should treat her with respect," Darcy said sharply.

Hearing the tone in her voice, Ben stopped messing about straight away. "Sorry, Dumpling," he said sweetly.

The lesson started and, as usual, the young riders walked, trotted and cantered around the indoor school with Vicki watching. She stood in the middle of the circle, correcting everybody's positions.

"Shoulders back, grip with your knees, heels down," she called out.

At first Darcy was concentrating so hard on keeping Ben under control she didn't think about Dumpling – these Saturday lessons were harder than she'd realized! But as Dumpling broke from a trot into a canter, Darcy suddenly realized that there was something wrong with the old Shetland. Her breathing was ragged and her head drooped as if she was tired. Tightening her grip on Dumpling's bridle, she called out, "Whoa, girl!"

The pony seemed more than happy to stop, and Darcy could see her barrel chest heaving as if she was fighting for breath. Darcy panicked and looked round to get Vicki's attention.

Looking concerned, Vicki came hurrying over. "What's the matter?" she asked.

"Dumpling's not right at all," Darcy said quickly. "Maybe she's got the flu like Mel."

Vicki ran her hand softly along Dumpling's neck. "Aren't you feeling well, sweetheart?" she whispered. In answer, the pony put her head against Vicki's chest and sighed heavily. Vicki quickly lifted Ben out of the saddle and put him firmly down on the ground.

"Sorry, but Dumpling's not feeling well today, Ben. We'll have to find you another pony to ride," she told the little boy, who looked as if he might have a tantrum.

As Darcy led Dumpling out of the indoor school, she heard Vicki say to Ben, "I promise you can ride Dumpling next week."

★

The riding lesson finished at ten o'clock but there were another two straight after it so it wasn't until after twelve that Vicki was free to check on Dumpling. Leaving Jess, Amber, Sam and Cara untacking their ponies, she hurried over to the field where Darcy had left Dumpling. Darcy ran behind Vicki, trying to keep up. Seeing her tense face, Darcy tried to make her smile.

"Dumpling will stuff her face with anything — maybe it's just a bit of colic?" she suggested.

Vicki shook her head. "It didn't look like colic — poor Dumpling just looked exhausted," she sighed.

When they got to the field, they found Dumpling lying down on the frosty grass. She struggled to get to her feet when she saw her mistress.

"Hello, babes!" Vicki said softly.

Tears came into Darcy's eyes as she watched Vicki kiss and cuddle the old pony. Vicki picked up Dumpling's bridle, which Darcy had left hanging on the gate, and put it on the pony.

"I'm going to tuck you up in your stable and give you a nice warm bran mash," she said gently.

Darcy clipped the lead rope onto Dumpling's bridle, then Vicki led the tired little pony across the yard to her stable.

As soon as Jess, Amber, Sam and Cara had turned their ponies out into the meadow for a well-deserved rest, they ran over to see Dumpling. She was in her stable now, settled down on a deep bed of straw. Darcy had filled up her hay-net and water bucket and Vicki had mixed her a bran mash, but it was standing untouched in the corner of the stable.

"It's the first time I've ever seen Dumpling ignore her food," Amber said in a worried voice. The rest of the girls nodded. Normally Dumpling would have gobbled her food down then kicked over the feed bucket, which was her way of saying, *More please*!

As usual, Sam tried to cheer everyone up. "A lesson with little Ben sitting on you would put anybody off their dinner!" she joked.

"Yeah," Jess agreed. "Maybe she just needs a good rest. She's well old."

Vicki just shook her head as if she was

puzzled. "I've never seen her so dopey before," she said, frowning.

"Are you going to call the vet, Vicki?" Amber asked.

Vicki nodded. "If she's no better in the morning, I'll definitely call her," she replied.

Cara's big blue eyes filled with tears as she blurted out, "I really hope she gets well soon."

★

Saturday afternoon was normally a time when the girls could get lots of their jobs done. With no visitors or children around, they could hose down the yard, re-stock the feed bins and clean their tack. But this afternoon they didn't get as much done as usual because they were so worried about Dumpling.

Darcy knew how important the little pony was to Vicki. All the girls knew the story of how she had got the Shetland when

she was only five. They'd gone to every
gymkhana they could. Dumpling was a
brilliant jumper and she nearly always came
away with a winning rosette fluttering on
her bridle. When Vicki outgrew Dumpling,
she moved on to Flora. But she had never
sold Dumpling; she kept her as a pet, letting
other little children learn to ride on her just
like she'd done.

Before the girls left for the night, they
stuck their heads over Dumpling's stable
door. She was snoozing in her deep straw
bed and blinked sleepily when she saw their
smiling faces.

"Sleep tight,"
Amber whispered.

Darcy blew Dumpling
a kiss and said softly,
"See you in the morning,
sweetheart."

Chapter 2

Darcy got her mum to drop her off at the stables early the next morning. She'd dreamed about Dumpling all night and wanted to see if she was OK. In the yard, she was surprised to see Mel.

"I didn't think I'd see you today!" She smiled at her friend. "Are you feeling better?"

Mel shrugged and grinned. "Not really, but I couldn't stay stuck in bed any longer," she said with a laugh. "I was soooo bored!"

When Darcy told her friend how poorly Dumpling had been during the riding lesson, Mel frowned.

"Oh no! Poor baby – let's go and see how she is," she said quickly.

But as the girls set off towards Dumpling's stable, Vicki appeared at her office door. "Can I see you for a minute?" she called out to them.

As they hurried over, the girls noticed that Vicki was still wearing a pink fleecy dressing gown.

"Maybe Vicki's ill like you've been," Darcy murmured. "I've never seen her walking round in her dressing gown before."

Mel screwed up her face. "I hope, for her sake, she *hasn't* caught this flu. I've felt really rough all week," she said.

As soon as they walked into the office they could see that something was wrong. Vicki's pretty face was pale and puffy and her eyes were all red and swollen.

"I've got bad news, girls," she blurted out.

Darcy's tummy started to feel funny – had something happened to one of her friends? She saw that Vicki was struggling to hold back her tears,

"Dumpling died last night," Vicki told them, her voice shaking.

Darcy gasped and grabbed hold of Mel's arm for support. Both girls were shocked and couldn't speak. They just stared at Vicki, who had started to cry now. "As soon

as it was light I went over to check on her.
At first I thought she was fast asleep, but
when I called her name, she didn't look up
like she normally does. I went into the stable
but she still didn't move – she was just lying
there looking really quiet and peaceful."

By this time Mel and Darcy were sobbing
too.

Vicki picked up a box of tissues and
handed it to them. "I'm sorry, I know it's a
big shock," she gulped.

The girls nodded and wiped their eyes as they tried to take in the awful news. Vicki was obviously gutted too but she was so kind — even now she was worrying about the girls.

"The vet's already on her way," she told them. She looked down at her dressing gown and managed a bit of a smile. "I'd better get changed before she gets here."

Mel and Darcy went out into the yard to wait for the rest of their friends to arrive. Mel kept shaking her head as if she couldn't take in the news.

"I can't believe it. I saw Dumpling yesterday just before I left and now I'll never see her again," she gasped.

Darcy nodded. "I can't get my head round it. I knew she was old, but I really thought she just had bad colic," she said.

They stopped talking suddenly when they heard Jess, Amber, Sam and Cara coming.

They were all laughing and giggling as if they didn't have a care in the world.

Darcy covered her mouth with her hands. "Oh no! How are we going to tell them?" she whispered nervously.

Mel coughed. "It's gonna be awful!" she said.

The four girls turned the corner and waved to their friends. But as soon as they saw Mel and Darcy's faces, they realized that something was wrong. They came running across the yard.

"What's up?" Amber asked.

Mel opened her mouth to speak but she just couldn't bring herself to tell them, so Darcy took a deep breath and stared hard at the ground before finally blurting out, "Guys . . . Dumpling died in the night."

Cara immediately started to sob; Sam buried her face in her hands; Amber just stared at Mel and Darcy in total disbelief; and Jess went red in the face and said over and over again, "No . . . no . . . no!"

When Vicki reappeared in her jeans and sweatshirt, she took one look at the crying girls and led them straight into the tack room, where she made mugs of tea with lots of sugar.

As the girls gulped down their warm drinks, the puppies, Treasure and Hunt, scampered in, excitedly wagging their tails. Amber and Mel had rescued them from drowning during a treasure hunt earlier in the year – and just seeing them cheered the girls up.

"We've all got to pull ourselves together," Vicki told them firmly. The girls nodded at her, but none of them spoke. "The vet will be here any minute to examine Dumpling and take her away." Vicki's voice was a bit wobbly now.

"Where will she go?" Cara asked, her voice faint.

Vicki quickly wiped the tears from her eyes and said, "I'll have her cremated and then scatter her ashes in the pony meadow."

"Oh yes. It's the place she loved most of all," Darcy gulped.

Vicki went across to the tack-room door. "Now, the best thing for you girls to do is sort out your ponies as usual," she said.

Amber took a deep breath. "They'll probably be able to tell that something's wrong," she said nervously.

Vicki nodded as she opened the door. "I'm sure they'll pick up on your mood, so be as brave as you can," she told them.

The ponies definitely knew there was something wrong. Beanz was even more skittish than usual, Candy shied at the slightest thing, Taffy seemed sad, Rose and Stella seemed confused, and Duke just stared at Darcy with his big, dark, intelligent eyes.

Darcy talked softly to him as she

groomed him. "Dumpling's not going to be around to play any more, babe," she said. When Duke heard his mistress's sad voice, he blew softly into her hair.

"I know you'll miss her, Duke. I will too, but she was a very old lady." Duke seemed to be listening carefully to every word Darcy was saying, and talking to him made her feel better. By the time she'd finished brushing him she felt stronger and calmer and Duke didn't look as sad either.

As Darcy was about to lead Duke out into the yard, she heard Henrietta Reece-Thomas and Camilla Worthington talking to each other in the next-door stable.

Henrietta owned President, a gorgeous spotty grey Appaloosa – he'd been a surprise birthday present from her rich parents. Camilla Worthington was the owner of Cleopatra, a crazy Arab pony with a very bad temper. Everybody except Vicki was scared of Cleo, even Camilla! Darcy thought it was sad. She could never imagine being scared of Duke!

Unlike Darcy, Henrietta and Camilla thought they were miles better than everybody else. They treated the yard girls like dirt and bossed them around all the time. They'd both stopped talking to Darcy since she'd made friends with the other girls, but Darcy didn't care. She hated the way they treated their ponies. Neither of them ever showed Cleo or President any love or gave them a kiss or a cuddle. They didn't ride very often – and they certainly never mucked their ponies out or groomed them;

it was a miracle if they even remembered to fill up their water buckets!

Darcy had to admit she didn't like moody Cleo, but she loved President and felt really sorry for him. He was such a gorgeous pony. When Henrietta was out of the way, Darcy and her friends would often sneak into his stable and slip him an apple or a carrot or half a packet of mints!

Darcy stopped dead when she heard Henrietta.

"Such a lot of fuss over a fat old pony that was way past its sell-by date anyway," she was saying to Camilla.

Camilla laughed. She was scared to death of Henrietta and did exactly what she told her. "Trust the stupid yard girls to milk it for all they can," she sneered.

Darcy was fuming. Before she could stop herself she had stomped into President's stable, where the snooty livery girls were still slagging off her friends.

"How dare you!" Darcy yelled at them.

Henrietta and Camilla jumped in surprise. "How dare *you* listen in on our private conversation," Henrietta hissed.

Darcy looked daggers at her. "I don't need to listen in when *you're* talking – you've got such a big mouth I can hear you even when I don't want to," she snapped.

Camilla gave her a dirty look. "Run away and play with your loser friends and their scummy little borrowed ponies," she mocked.

Darcy wanted to smack them both but

she took a deep breath and said, "If I hear you saying anything about Dumpling again, I'll repeat every single word to Vicki, and with a bit of luck she'll kick the pair of you out of her yard!" Then she stormed back to Duke's stable.

★

Later, Darcy and her friends turned their ponies out into the pony meadow, then went to the tack room to clean their tack. Seeing Dumpling's saddle and bridle hanging up on the wall brought a lump to their throats. They fought back their tears though and tried to think about all the happy times they'd had with the cheeky little Shetland pony.

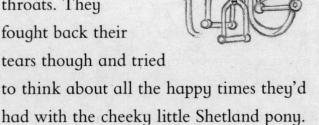

When they were just finishing off the
tack, a large van drove into the yard – the
girls knew it had come to take Dumpling to
the crematorium.

Cara turned pale at the sight of it and
her big blue eyes filled with tears. "I *so* don't
want to watch this!" she blurted out.

The other girls nodded.

"Let's go into the pony meadow till it's all over," Darcy suggested quickly.

As they were hurrying across the yard, they passed Vicki, wrapped up in a warm fleece. She was pale, but she looked calmer now. "I'm going to go with Dumpling," she told them quickly. "Then I can say goodbye to her properly."

Darcy couldn't believe how strong Vicki was. She was going to stay with her pony right up until the end.

Seeing their sad faces, Vicki said softly, "The vet told me that Dumpling died of a heart attack due to old age. She said that she would have gone very quickly and not suffered any pain, so we can be grateful for that."

Vicki's words did make the girls feel a bit better and they headed quietly for the pony meadow. The ponies were surprised to see them back so soon and came over for a treat or a cuddle.

Darcy buried her face in Duke's neck. "I'm really glad Dumpling didn't suffer," she said softly.

Amber sighed heavily as she stroked Stella's pretty white blaze. "We'll miss her loads," she mumbled, and Stella nudged her arm as if to say, *We'll miss her too.*

Sam gave Beanz a mint so that he'd stop butting her in the tummy. "The Saturday morning riders will be *well* upset when they hear that Dumpling died," she said.

Mel looked up from kissing Candy's velvety soft muzzle. "I hadn't thought about them at all. They're going to miss her *so* much."

Jess was running her fingers through Rose's silky silver mane; she looked thoughtful. "I suppose Vicki will have to think about getting another pony soon, then," she said.

Cara chewed on her fingernails, something she always did when she was worried. "We owe Vicki so much . . . I wish we could do something to help her."

Amber nodded. "By letting us look after her ponies she's made all our dreams come true," she agreed.

Darcy was thinking hard. Vicki hadn't needed to give her a pony to look after because she already had Duke, but she was amazing and Darcy loved her just as much as the other girls did. She suddenly looked up and smiled. "We *can* do something – we can help her buy another pony," she cried.

The other girls stared at her in amazement.

"How are we going to raise that much money?" Mel spluttered.

"I don't mean hundreds of pounds, I just mean a contribution *towards* a new pony," Darcy explained.

Cara smiled sweetly. "I've been saving up my pocket money all year," she said shyly. "I'll definitely give that."

Jess grinned at her. "That's dead sweet,

Car, but maybe it should be something we can do all together," she said.

Mel looked thoughtful. "Pity it's not spring or autumn when everybody's organizing sponsored rides – we could make loads of money doing one of those," she said.

"We could have a car boot sale in the yard," Amber suggested, but Sam burst out laughing.

"You wouldn't make a penny from the rubbish I've got!" she giggled.

There was silence for a while as all the girls thought hard.

Suddenly Darcy grinned and clicked her fingers. "There is *something* we can do," she announced.

The others turned to her. "What?" they said all at the same time.

Darcy laughed and looked round at their faces. "We can go carol singing on Christmas Eve!"

Chapter 3

Jess, Amber, Mel, Sam and Cara all looked
at Darcy as if she was mad.

"*Carol singing!*" they laughed.

"On Christmas Eve? That's only the day
after tomorrow," Amber said.

Darcy grinned at them and nodded.
"I know, but I think it will work. Carol
singing – with a difference! We could sing
carols on our ponies in the market square!"

They were quiet for a few seconds, then
Mel said, "You know, it's a wicked idea! I
think we should do it!"

"We could dress up all Christmassy," said
Amber excitedly.

"I wonder if there's any way we could hold candles or something," Jess thought out loud.

Cara looked nervous. "Hang on a minute – that doesn't sound very safe. I'm not sure I can carry a candle and hold onto Taffy's reins without setting myself on fire," she said.

Darcy put her arm round her and smiled. "Don't worry, Car, we'll work something out."

The girls planned their idea all afternoon. They'd ride over to the market place on Christmas Eve afternoon, arriving at about four o'clock, just as it was starting to get dark.

"We could wear Santa hats over our riding hats," said Mel, clapping her hands.

Sam nodded. "And we could decorate the ponies' bridles with tinsel," she added.

Cara was still looking worried though. "I don't know that many carols," she admitted.

Sam pulled a funny face. "Well . . . do you want my good news or my bad news?" she asked.

"Bad news first," Mel said.

"I can't sing in tune!" Sam giggled.

"And the good news?" Amber asked with a smile.

"I do know 'Rudolph the Red-Nosed Reindeer' all the way through!"

★

When Vicki drove into the yard later that day, she looked pale and exhausted.

"Shall we tell Vicki what we're planning to do?" Darcy asked her friends.

Jess shook her head. "She looks done in to me," she said.

Darcy nodded. "You're right; let's leave her alone for a bit and tell her just before we go home," she suggested.

It was an icy-cold afternoon, and when the girls went to collect their ponies from the meadow, they seemed really pleased to get back to their snug warm stables. Even Duke, who loved the outdoors most of all, dragged Darcy across the yard.

"Whoa there, boy," Darcy laughed as she ran to keep up with him. Back in the stable, she took off Duke's rug and groomed his thick winter coat until it shone. "Who's beautiful?" she whispered in his pretty pointed ears.

After she'd brushed Duke, Darcy put his rug back on to keep him warm during the frosty night. Then she gave him a bucket of pony nuts and a full hay-net which she tied to a loop on the wall. "There you are, sweetheart," she said as she gently patted him. Duke looked up from his supper and whinnied softly to say thank you! His warm breath steamed as it hit the cold frosty air and the stable smelled sweetly of the clean straw and his warm body.

All of a sudden Darcy heard Henrietta's loud voice again. She was in the next stable doing what she did best – having a go at someone.

"I can't believe how many times I've told you about topping up President's water bucket!" she was

shouting at Mel and Cara, who were on livery duty that week.

Darcy felt really sorry for her friends. She knew that

Cara was scared stiff of Henrietta, but luckily Mel was with her and she always stood up for herself.

"We always fill up his bucket but President knocks it over quite a lot," Mel snapped crossly.

Henrietta ignored her. "My father pays good money for my pony to be taken care of – I don't expect to have to tell you again," she shouted in her posh voice.

"Maybe you could get your hands dirty one day, you snotty idiot, and fill the bucket up yourself!" Darcy heard Mel scream. She smiled to herself. Trust Mel to challenge lazy Henrietta. She deserved it: she hardly lifted a finger when it came to looking after President.

"If it happens again, I shall get Daddy to have a word with Vicki about you," Henrietta threatened.

Darcy watched as Henrietta stomped out of President's stable and across the yard with her nose in the air. As soon as she was out of sight Darcy went and found her friends,

who were now in Cleopatra's stable. Cara
was standing in a corner looking pale and
Mel was coughing and struggling to put
Cleo's rug on her.

"Every time I try to throw the rug over
her she nips me," Mel grumbled in a croaky
voice.

"Let me help you," Darcy offered. "You're
obviously still not totally better," and she
took a firm hold of the moody Arab's
headcollar and held her tight while Mel
rugged her up.

"I'm fine – don't worry about me. It's just annoying. Cleo wouldn't be so vicious if stupid Camilla rode her more often," Mel grumbled as she fastened the straps round the pony's chest.

Darcy nodded. "It's just cruel to keep such a lively Arab cooped up all the time," she said crossly.

After the three of them had settled President and Cleopatra down for the night, they joined the rest of their friends, who were waiting for them in the dark yard. Feeling a bit nervous, they walked towards Vicki's office. There were no curtains in the window and they could see Vicki sitting at her desk.

Cara hesitated. "She looks shattered," she said nervously. "Maybe this is a bad idea."

But Darcy kept on walking. "We can't keep putting it off – Christmas Eve is the day after tomorrow!"

At first Vicki was shocked by the girls' idea, but they could see she was touched by their kindness. What none of them had expected was that she'd want to join in and help.

"Great. I'll drive down to the market square with flasks of hot chocolate and mince pies to warm everybody up," she insisted.

Sam grinned. "Cool! I love hot chocolate – and maybe you could bring our song sheets at the same time," she said cheekily.

"Oooh!" Vicki said, grinning like an excited little girl. "I've got some gorgeous lanterns you could carry. I lent them to Rob – you know, from the farm up the road – for a party he had, so we'd have to get them back, but they'd look gorgeous."

Now that the girls could see Vicki was pleased, they were even more keen on the idea.

"You'll have to wear a Father Christmas hat as well, Vicki," Darcy said with a giggle.

Vicki smiled for the first time that day. "I'd dress up as a big ugly bear for this if I had to!"

★

It was pitch dark by the time the girls left the stables, so Vicki walked with them

53

across the yard holding her
big powerful torch
in front of her.

"Thanks for being so
supportive today, girls," she
said. "I really appreciate it."

The girls all smiled
shyly, but it was Jess who
said what they were all thinking:

"You've given us so much – now we'd like
to try and help you out."

★

With Christmas Eve so close, the girls
couldn't waste any time. The next day they
met at the stables early before splitting up
to make sure all their jobs got done. Jess
and Amber were going shopping for tinsel
and Father Christmas hats, and Sam and
Cara were going to the library to look up
the words to some carols on the internet and
print them out.

Darcy's mum thought that they might need to get permission from the local authorities to sing in the market square so Darcy decided to hack over and ask at the council office.

Vicki nodded in agreement. "I should have thought of that straight away," she said. "We don't want to get arrested for illegal busking!"

Mel decided to go with Darcy. "I need to feel like I'm some use at the moment," she moaned. "Anyway, I reckon the fresh air will do me good."

Darcy suddenly remembered the lanterns. "Shall we stop off at Rob's farm on the way, Vicki?" she asked. "Then we can ask him about the lanterns and he can see if he can find them. We'll be all sorted then!"

"Good idea!" agreed Vicki. "Tell him I'll give him a call this afternoon to work out when's best for him to drop them off."

★

It was cold and windy when Mel and Darcy
set off along the frosty bridle path. The
ponies were just happy to be outside though,
and they sniffed the sharp air and tossed
their heads excitedly. At the end of the
bridleway Darcy and Mel relaxed their grip
on their reins and both ponies shot off across
an empty field, pounding the earth
with their hooves.

The cold air made the girls' cheeks glow.
When they reached the end of the field,
the ponies slowed down and Darcy and
Mel grinned at each other as they caught
their breath.

"Phew! That's got to be the best feeling
in the world," Darcy gasped.

Mel wiped her running nose. "Yep,
the best!" she agreed.

The girls had met Rob and his wife, Molly, quite a few times before because they supplied Vicki's yard with straw and hay. And as they pulled up at the farm gate, Molly arrived at the same time. She'd been out walking their dog, Baxter, and had bright-red cheeks, just like the girls.

"Girls! Hello!" she said with a smile. "What a lovely surprise. What can we do for you?"

The girls quickly dismounted and Mel bent down to stroke the beautiful sheepdog while Darcy explained about their fundraising idea and the lanterns.

Molly was really keen on their plan. "Oh, Darcy, that sounds lovely," she said. "We'll definitely try and pop along tomorrow. Now then, let's find Rob and ask about these lanterns." She led them across the farm to a little field beside the farmhouse, where Rob was watching a little grey donkey, who was grazing peacefully.

"How are you, girls?" he called over as soon as he saw them.

They quickly tied Candy and Duke to the fence and went to join him in the field. Molly explained what they'd come for.

"That's fine," Rob told them. "I can take the lanterns over to the stables at about two o'clock. I'll give Vicki a ring and let her know."

He crouched down to pet the donkey. "Now, what do you think of Daisy, the lovely new addition to our farm?" he asked.

"Rob got her as an early Christmas present to himself!" Molly laughed.

"She's gorgeous!" cried Darcy. And both girls gave Daisy a big hug. She had a thick woolly coat; she nuzzled their hands and Mel gave her some of the mints she had in her jeans pockets.

As the donkey happily crunched the mints, Rob patted her round belly. "She's a bit podgy, but I suppose she needs a bit of fat on her to keep her warm through the winter," he said with a laugh.

The girls gave Daisy a final cuddle, then said goodbye and thanks to Rob and Molly and set off again for the village, singing "Little Donkey" at the tops of their voices.

Chapter 4

Mel and Darcy got permission for the girls to sing, but Christmas Eve turned out to be the coldest day of the year and Mel arrived at the stables looking worse than ever.

"It's so annoying," she said. "I just can't get rid of this stupid flu."

"You shouldn't be out in this weather," Darcy told her.

Mel shook her head and looked very stubborn. "There's no *way* I'm missing out on today," she insisted.

Sam turned up wearing two scarves and two pairs of gloves. "I hate being cold – I've got so many clothes on I look like a sumo wrestler!" she said with a laugh.

"You'll need them – the temperature's gonna fall below zero tonight," said Amber.

Before the girls set off, they wrapped sparkly tinsel round their saddles and bridles, then pulled on the fluffy red and white Christmas hats on top of their riding hats.

"We look like Santa's little helpers!" joked Sam.

Sensing that the girls were excited, the ponies stamped their feet and chewed impatiently on their bits.

"OK, guys, calm it, we'll be off soon," Jess promised.

Vicki packed their lanterns and song sheets into the boot of her old Jeep, along with boxes of mince pies and some flasks of hot chocolate. "See you in town," she told them.

The girls smiled and set off in their luminous riding gear.

"Vicki seems almost as excited as we are," said Amber as they turned out of the yard.

Darcy nodded. "Maybe this fundraising idea has given her something apart from

Dumpling to think about."

Sam grinned as frisky Beanz started off at a brisk trot. "We've got to sing our socks off tonight," she said with a laugh. "Then we'll make loads of money."

Darcy and Mel had told their friends about Daisy the donkey and the girls couldn't resist stopping off at the farm to say hello to her on the way to the market place. She wasn't as lively as she'd been the day before. Instead of trotting up to say hello, she plodded slowly towards the fence, where she stood looking very subdued. Cara, Jess, Amber and Sam thought she was gorgeous but Mel and Darcy were surprised by how different she seemed.

"She wasn't like this yesterday," Darcy said, frowning.

"Maybe she's tired?" Amber suggested.

Sam shivered and then giggled. "Or just freezing cold like I am," she said.

Darcy gave Daisy a gentle pat and promised, "We'll check you out on our way back."

★

By the time they reached the town centre it was dark, but the market square looked stunning: fairy lights twinkled from the lampposts and the huge Christmas tree. With the help of some of the Saturday morning riders and Susie, her assistant at the stables, Vicki had set up a table, lit it with lanterns and laid out her mince pies and hot chocolate.

When the crowds of shoppers saw the
ponies come clip-clopping into the
market place, they stopped and gathered
round.

"I feel like a famous celebrity!"
joked Sam.

The girls lined up so that they faced the crowd, who were smiling at them as they waited to hear what the girls were going to do. Their families were there too, waving enthusiastically, wrapped up in woolly hats, gloves and scarves.

Darcy had spotted her mum and dad and Annabelle straight away, and she could see Amber's mum and dad standing near Cara's mum. Jess and Sam's mums and brothers were there too, but she couldn't see any of Mel's family. She leaned over and whispered in Mel's ear, "Are your dad and the boys not coming, Mel?"

Mel grinned cheekily. "No. I've given Dad and Kyle this stupid flu so they're staying in the warm, and Kalvin didn't want to come on his own. I'm not bothered anyway," she said. "It would just make me more nervous!"

"I'm so nervous I think I might forget the words to the songs!" Cara gulped.

Darcy spoke to the crowd before they all got total stage fright. She took a deep breath and looked over at her mum and dad. They both gave her a thumbs-up and Annabelle waved as hard as she could. "Merry Christmas, everybody!" Darcy called out.

"We're here to raise funds for Vicki's Riding School – we hope you'll give generously."

The girls nervously started to sing the "The Holly and the Ivy", and the crowd started to join in straight away, which made them all feel better. Vicki and her helpers handed out song sheets to everybody, and the sound of over fifty happy voices in the cold frosty night air made Darcy shiver with excitement.

The mood got better with every song the girls performed. Coins jingled in the collection boxes as they sang their way through "Rudolph the Red-Nosed Reindeer" and "Jingle Bells". But the song that stole the show was "Little Donkey". They began to sing just as snowflakes started to flutter down from the dark sky.

"More, more!" yelled the crowd.

"More 'Little Donkey'!" insisted a little boy.

Darcy glanced over at Mel: she looked shattered. "I can't sing another word – my throat's killing me," she croaked.

Darcy gave her a pat on the arm. "Just mime it, babe. This has got to be the last song anyway," she said.

So all the girls, except poor Mel, sang it again, and by the time they'd finished the snow was beginning to settle in places. Before the shoppers left, Vicki offered everybody mince pies and hot chocolate, and the cold, hungry girls stuffed their faces too! The pies were rich and spicy and the hot chocolate was delicious.

"Mmmm, just what I needed," said Darcy through a mouthful of pie.

People in the crowd came up and thanked them for the carols, and little children gathered round the ponies, who stood patiently under the falling snow.

The girls all said goodbye to their families, who were planning to drive to the stables and then take them home after they had ridden their ponies back.

Vicki told the girls not to hang around for too long. "I'm worried about you hacking back in the snow – it's falling pretty fast now and the bridle paths will be slippery," she warned.

"We'll be fine," said Jess. "And Darcy and Sam have got their mobiles with them in case we need anything."

By now Mel was coughing her head off. "Are you well enough to ride back?" Vicki asked her.

Tough little Mel nodded firmly. "Yes, I'm fine," she croaked in a low whisper.

But Darcy knew that she was in no state
to hack back in the freezing cold. "You
don't sound fine, Mel," she said. "I think
you should go home with Vicki."

At first Mel
looked a bit
annoyed but
she didn't have
the energy to
argue. "Maybe
you're right.
Will one of you
be OK leading
Candy back?"
she asked.

The others all nodded.

"We'll take it in turns to lead her," Jess
said.

Mel slowly dismounted, then slumped into
the front seat of Vicki's old Jeep. "Thank
you," she gasped.

Her friends took off their christmas hats zipped up their jackets and then mounted their ponies, who were covered in snow.

"Keep your torches on when you get onto the bridleway," Vicki called after them.

"Don't worry – we will," Darcy called back as they trotted out of the market square, leaving the bright Christmas lights twinkling behind them.

★

The ride back was a lot quieter. On the way there they'd all been practising their Christmas carols but now the snow was falling fast, and a bitterly cold wind made them crouch low in their saddles to keep warm. The ponies were tired and they were quiet too – except Beanz, of course, who kept shying at the snowflakes that drifted past his eyes. Sam was tugging hard on his reins but she was having a real struggle stopping him from bolting.

"He hates the snow," she said.

Jess, who was leading Candy, sighed wearily. "I'll be glad when we get back to the yard," she said.

As they got near to Rob's farm, they heard a braying sound in the distance.

Darcy tugged at her reins to halt Duke. "Daisy doesn't sound too happy," she said in a worried voice.

Amber looked concerned too – she loved all animals and hated to see them suffer. "I think we should go and check she's OK," she said quickly.

They trotted over to Daisy's field and found the donkey lying down in the snow. When she saw them, she tried to stagger to her feet but she couldn't get up.

"Poor thing, she must be ill!" cried Cara.

Darcy turned Duke and headed towards the farmhouse. "I'll just go and get Rob," she called as she trotted off.

While she was gone, the girls patted and stroked Daisy but she kept making little grunting noises.

"She sounds like she's in loads of pain," said Amber tensely.

They were relieved when they heard Duke trotting back towards them, but then, when they saw Darcy's face, they started to panic.

"No one's at home – the house is totally dark," she told her friends, frowning.

They all just looked at each other for a minute.

"Maybe they've gone away for Christmas," Jess cried.

But Darcy shook her head. "No – Molly mentioned that they might try and come today so they must be around. And I don't think Rob would leave Daisy on her own for long," she reasoned.

Sam agreed. "They might be out celebrating – it *is* Christmas Eve," she said.

Amber spoke quickly. "We can't leave Daisy like this – we've got to get help *now*," she said.

Darcy took her phone out of her pocket. "I'll phone Vicki – she'll know what to do," she said. The girls waited while she dialled.

Darcy frowned. "I can't get any signal," she told them.

Then Sam tried using her mobile, but she couldn't get a signal either. Cara burst into tears. Her sobs and Daisy's painful little noises made Darcy realize that they had to do something.

"I could ride over to the vet's house – it's only about a mile away," she said.

Jess frowned. "No way are you going on your own."

"It's OK, really. I've got my phone – maybe I'll get a signal somewhere else – and I know the way," Darcy said firmly.

This time it was Sam who argued with her. "No. It's not safe – I'll come with you," she offered.

Darcy couldn't help but smile at the idea. "Sammy, Beanz *hates* the snow!" she pointed out. "It would take us half an hour to get to the end of the farm track!"

Sam nodded. "I s'pose I can't argue with that," she replied.

"No," Jess insisted. "You can't go on your own. One of us is coming with you."

Cara's blue eyes filled with tears. "Please don't make *me* go," she said.

"There's no need for you to go, Car," Amber told her. "Either me or Jess can go."

Darcy shook her head. "Honestly, guys, I'll be fine," she said. "It's slippery, Amber, and you can't risk breaking that arm again. You might never be able to ride again."

"Fine," Jess said stubbornly. "I'll come with you."

"Look," said Darcy. "It would be fine if Mel was here – she's the fastest rider. But she's not here and I'm the next fastest. And by the look of Daisy I need to get to the vet as quickly as possible. Don't take this the wrong way, Jess, but you'll slow me down. Rose doesn't like the snow very much either, and she's so pale she's really hard to see when it's like this. It could be dangerous."

"Well . . . We're just wasting time standing around here in the freezing cold arguing, I suppose," Jess reasoned. "As long as you're sure."

Sam looked at Darcy. "I don't know what else we can do. But be careful," she begged.

Darcy nodded, then, turning Duke, she trotted off through the dark snowy night, holding a torch to guide her on her way.

Chapter 5

Darcy cantered as fast as she dared, but she knew she had to be careful because it was so dark and icy. She didn't want to spend Christmas Day in hospital with a broken leg, and she certainly didn't want Duke to get hurt. As she rode through the dark night, with snow swirling into her face, Darcy was really worrying.

What if, after all this, the vet wasn't in?
She might be out at a Christmas party.
Darcy felt almost sick with fear. Maybe
she should have just ridden straight back
to Vicki's yard in the first place . . . ?

She needed to calm down so she pulled
Duke up and tried to call Vicki again. She
soon realized that there was still no signal.
Feeling cold, scared and very alone, Darcy
decided that the best thing was to carry on.
So she gritted her teeth and rode onwards
through the snow.

★

As Darcy battled her way to the vet's,
Jess, Amber, Sam and Cara were beginning
to panic too. Daisy had suddenly got
much worse. Her breathing was ragged
and her stomach was heaving up and
down.

"Oh no! She looks just like Dumpling did
before she died!" cried Amber.

Cara put her head in her hands. "Please don't let her die too," she sobbed. "It's Christmas and everything's supposed to be happy."

Sam took out her mobile and tried Vicki again, but she *still* couldn't get a signal. She wondered if maybe she should go up to the farm and see if the reception was any better up there.

"What are we going to do?" Jess asked.

Amber looked serious. "Cross our fingers that Darcy makes it to the vet's house, I s'pose. Otherwise we're in big trouble."

★

Darcy gasped in surprise as the surface under Duke's feet changed. They were now on a road and she smiled to herself. It was much safer and easier to ride on than the bridleway, and lorries had obviously been round to grit it earlier in the day so it wasn't as slippery. Taking a deep breath, she held out her torch and stared through the snow. She could see lights twinkling in the distance.

"Yes!" she shouted. "We made it, baby!" Duke tossed his dark mane, now covered with snow, and trotted briskly towards the village where the vet lived.

Darcy nearly burst into tears when she finally arrived and found the vet at home. She was stuffing the turkey for her family's Christmas dinner! Darcy stammered out an apology, then told the vet about Daisy lying ill in the field at the farm.

The vet quickly washed her hands, then grabbed her coat and car keys. "Are you all right to ride back to Vicki's yard?" she asked before she left.

Darcy nodded. "I'll be fine," she answered – although it was the very last thing she wanted to do. She was shattered, and scared at the thought of having to get back onto the icy bridleway that she'd just left behind her! But she took a deep breath and pulled herself together. "Come on, Darcy," she told herself. "Nearly done. You can do this."

★

Meanwhile, Vicki was frantic. She'd dropped Mel off at her house, then gone back to the yard, where the girls' families were waiting. Sam and Darcy's parents had been trying to call them every few minutes, but for some reason they weren't answering their mobile phones. Vicki couldn't get

hold of them from her land line, either.
Eventually she jumped back into the Jeep
and set off to find them.

Vicki drove slowly along the track that
the girls had taken. All the time she drove she
tried to get hold of them using her hands-free
set. Dialling Sam's number once more, she
finally heard it ringing and gasped with relief
when she heard her voice on the other end.

"Sam! Where are you, sweetie?" she cried.

There was a crackle on the line, then
Sam said faintly, "At Rob's farm – Daisy
the donkey's really ill, Vicki."

Vicki sped up. "I'll be with you as quickly
as I can," she shouted.

By the time she got there, the farm tracks
were covered with deep snow. She found
Jess, Amber, Sam and Cara shivering with
cold and huddled round Daisy, trying to
keep her warm. Vicki crouched down beside
the donkey, shining her torch along her

body and feeling her heaving tummy.

"Oh, my goodness, she's in labour!" she gasped.

The girls were so shocked they could hardly speak. It was Sam who found her voice first.

"She's having a baby!" she squeaked.

Vicki nodded. "Yes ... . and by the looks of it, it'll be here very soon," she said urgently. She looked up at the girls. "Where are Rob and Molly?" she asked.

"They're not in – we've been going over to check every ten minutes," said Amber.

"We tried phoning the vet but we couldn't get a signal so Darcy rode over to fetch her," Jess said breathlessly.

Vicki looked alarmed. "She rode over in this snowstorm? Alone?" she cried.

"We're so sorry, Vicki. We didn't know what else to do," Cara said frantically.

Everybody – even Vicki – was panicking now. But just as they started to think that Daisy might die too, headlights shone at the end of the farm track. They all held their breath as a four-wheel drive with a trailer bouncing along behind it came skidding and sliding through the snow.

Vicki let out a sigh of relief when the driver's door swung open and the vet jumped out.

"Thank goodness!" she said weakly.

The vet took one look at Daisy and then started to shout out a list of instructions to Vicki. Vicki did what she was told and then positioned herself behind Daisy while the vet crouched next to the donkey's bloated belly. Daisy grunted in pain, and sensitive Amber quickly said, "Guys, we're not gonna be much help and we'll probably just get in the way. Let's get out of here."

The girls huddled round their ponies for warmth – they were now totally covered in snow. Beanz nuzzled Sam's cold hands and Rose blew warm air onto Jess's freezing face. Cara pressed her nose into Taffy's thick, blond mane.

"I hope Daisy will be all right," she said tearfully.

★

After only about twenty minutes the vet called out, "Girls . . . you can come over now." They hurried back to the field and found Daisy standing up. She was licking her new-born foal, which was wobbling on its long skinny legs.

"It's a boy!" Vicki cried.

The vet smiled at the girls. "It was a breech birth, which can be very dangerous for both mother and baby," she said. "Really well done. Daisy would have died if you hadn't acted so quickly."

Jess, Amber, Sam and Cara smiled at each other.

"It's Darcy who's the real hero!" said Amber proudly.

"I hope she's OK though," Cara said, frowning.

The vet said that Daisy and her little colt had to get indoors as soon as possible. The farm did have a few outbuildings but

they were all locked. Vicki offered to let
Daisy and the baby have a warm stable at
her yard if the vet could drive them there
in her trailer, and she willingly agreed. She
carefully picked up the little foal, carried
him into her trailer
and settled him
down on a
pile of straw.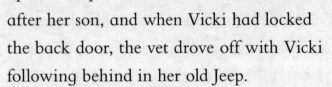
Daisy trotted
up the ramp
after her son, and when Vicki had locked
the back door, the vet drove off with Vicki
following behind in her old Jeep.

Jess, Amber, Sam and Cara would've
loved a ride home in the warm comfy
car. But there was no way any of them
would have left their ponies behind, so they
mounted up and, with Amber now leading
Candy, encouraged their cold, tired ponies
to set off again down the dark, snowy track.

Chapter 6

Darcy got back to the yard just minutes
before the vet drove in, quickly followed
by Vicki. Vicki jumped out of her Jeep as
soon as she saw Darcy standing by Duke,
shivering with cold and exhaustion. Darcy's
mum and dad were with her. Her dad was
carrying Annabelle, who was asleep with
her head on his shoulder, but Darcy's mum
had her arms round her daughter to try and
get her warm again.

"Are you OK?" Vicki asked anxiously.

Darcy nodded but couldn't say very
much. "Cold but OK," she replied.

The vet came over to say hello again.

"I just told your friends back there that if you hadn't acted so quickly, Daisy would probably have died," she said to Darcy. "You're a brave girl."

Darcy's dad looked at her and smiled. "We're so proud of you, darling."

Darcy shrugged. "We had to do something," she said, blushing. "Is Daisy all right?" she asked.

Both Vicki and the vet nodded quickly. "She's fine now," the vet replied.

Vicki winked as she opened the back door of the trailer. "Darcy, come over here," she called mysteriously. "Take a look for yourself."

Darcy couldn't believe her eyes when she peeped inside the trailer and saw not one but *two* donkeys! "Wow!" she gasped in amazement.

The vet let down the ramp and Daisy wobbled down it. Her baby followed. He was wobbly too, but as soon as his feet touched solid ground he gave a little kick, then skipped over to his mum, who nuzzled him lovingly.

Vicki turned to Darcy. "I know you're shattered, babe, but can you help me settle them down in Dumpling's stable before you go home? I'm going to look after them both until Rob gets back," she said.

Vicki and Darcy watched Daisy snuggle down on a deep bed of straw with her fluffy little foal at her side.

"I know Dumpling would be happy to share her stable with these two tonight," Vicki said softly.

Darcy wanted to cry as she stared in wonder at the little foal, who was drinking his mother's milk hungrily. "They look like a picture on a Christmas card," she said.

Vicki laughed as she brushed snow off her soaking fleece. "And you look like the abominable snowman!" she said. "You need to get into some dry clothes as soon as you can."

While her mum and dad took Annabelle back to the car to wait, Darcy quickly led Duke into his stable. She untacked him and dried him down before putting on his rug for the night.

She was just mixing him a warm bran

mash in the feed room when Jess, Amber, Sam and Cara came trotting into the yard, covered in snow from head to toe. Hearing the sound of the ponies' hooves, Darcy rushed out to meet them.

"Here's our hero! You're such a star, Darcy!" Amber said as soon as she saw her.

"I didn't have a clue that Daisy was in labour!" Darcy said with a laugh.

"I know, we couldn't believe it either," laughed Sam. "What will Mel say when we tell her?"

Cara dismounted stiffly, and after giving her mum a big hug, she brushed a thick layer of snow from Taffy's pretty little nose. "Time for a warm bran mash," she whispered.

Sam grinned. "That sounds so good I could eat it myself!"

Finally all the ponies were tucked up in their stables with a full bucket of water, a fresh hay-net and a bran mash to get stuck into. Duke whinnied loudly to say thank you to his brave mistress, then hungrily buried his head in his feed bucket.

Darcy kissed him goodnight and whispered, "You certainly deserve that, you little hero!"

On Christmas morning the girls turned up
at the yard as normal. They were still tired
but they all had Christmas presents for
their ponies.

Hearing their excited voices, the ponies
popped their heads over the half-doors
of their stables and whinnied loudly.
Darcy went into Duke's stable
and gave him a big hug.

"Merry Christmas,
gorgeous boy!" she
said. As well as the
new saddle rug,
Darcy had brought
Duke a basket full
of apples, carrots
and mints, and he
greedily attacked a
juicy apple which
Darcy held out to him.

Cara had bought Taffy a pink lead rope, and Amber had got Stella a new saddle rug too. Sam had saved up to buy Beanz some bright orange leg bandages and Jess had made a pony Christmas cake for Rose to share with her friends!

They were all laughing and gossiping with excitement as they opened the ponies' presents. Suddenly Mel walked into the yard and all the girls shrieked happily. She was wearing a big woolly blue scarf and looked a bit 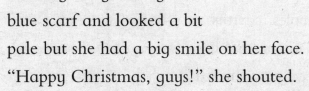 pale but she had a big smile on her face. "Happy Christmas, guys!" she shouted.

"Happy Christmas!" they called back to her as they ran over. Mel had bought a new blue tack box for Candy, along with three packets of her favourite mints. As she gave them to her, the rest of the girls excitedly filled Mel in on the adventures of the previous evening.

Darcy couldn't remember ever being this happy, but in the midst of all the noise she suddenly realized that there were two ponies who weren't having any fun. Henrietta and Camilla wouldn't dream of coming to the yard on Christmas Day – they were probably still in their pyjamas by the fire at home, and now President and Cleopatra looked very lonely. Seeing their sad faces over their stable doors made Darcy's soft heart ache.

"Father Christmas hasn't visited President and Cleo!" she called out to her friends.

Sam was the first to reply. "Then we'd better make sure that his little helpers make up for it!"

The girls filled two buckets with apples, carrots, mints and pony nuts, one for President and one for Cleo. The ponies started to neigh excitedly as the girls approached their stables. For the first time ever, Cleo was so happy she even forgot to bite anybody!

When they'd finished making a fuss of President and Cleopatra, the girls headed for the tack room, where they got the best Christmas present of all. Vicki came in with the collection tins. After giving them all a hug and a box of chocolates and wishing them a Happy Christmas, she smiled.

"You'll never believe how much we made yesterday," she said excitedly.

The girls all looked at her.

"Twenty quid?" Jess guessed.

Vicki shook her head and smiled as she rattled the tins. "Nearly a hundred pounds!" she cried.

Jess, Amber, Cara, Mel, Sam and Darcy gazed at each other in amazement.

"Maybe it was worth getting frozen to death after all!" joked Sam.

★

While the girls were mucking out the stables half an hour later, Rob came zooming into

103

the yard in his car. Vicki had posted a note
through his letter box the evening before
to explain what had happened. Now she
greeted him with a twinkle in her grey eyes.

"Were you and Molly out partying all
night?" she asked
cheekily.

Rob
grimaced
and shook
his head.
"We
decided
to pop
over
to my
brother's for
lunch, but we got
stuck in the snowstorm on the motorway on
the way back," he replied. "We were there
for hours!"

Vicki smiled cheerfully. "Lucky my brave girls looked after your donkey then, eh?" she said.

Rob nodded and grinned at the girls, who had joined Vicki in the yard. "I really can't thank you enough," he said gratefully.

He smiled happily when the girls took him to see Daisy and her foal and he decided straight away that the little donkey should be called Darcy after the brave girl who had saved his life! "What an idiot I am – I thought Daisy was just fat!" he said with a chuckle.

Before Rob left the yard he gave the girls an envelope. "I'm sorry I had to miss your carol singing, but here's a little something to drop into your collection tin," he said with a wink.

When he'd gone, Darcy ripped open the envelope and gasped when she saw a cheque inside. "Thirty pounds!" she yelled.

Jess, Amber, Sam, Cara and Mel jumped up and down and hugged each other.

"Wow! We've made loads of money now!" Mel laughed.

Darcy waved the cheque around and grinned happily. "Well, we'll never ever forget Dumpling, but Vicki should be able to get a new pony soon," she said softly.

★

And Darcy was right. By the start of January there was a gorgeous new addition to Vicki's yard: a lovely five-year-old Shetland pony called Carol!

THE END